MINERVA LOUISE
at School

Janet Morgan Stoeke

SCHOLASTIC INC.
New York   Toronto   London   Auckland   Sydney
Mexico City   New Delhi   Hong Kong

For my mom and dad with love

Copyright © 1996 by Janet Morgan Stoeke.
All rights reserved. Published by Scholastic Inc., 555 Broadway, New York, NY 10012,
by arrangement with Dutton Children's Books, a division of Penguin Putnam Inc.
SCHOLASTIC and associated logos and designs are trademarks
and/or registered trademarks of Scholastic Inc.

Printed in the U.S.A.

ISBN 0-439-10577-3

10 09 08 07 06 05 04 03 02 01   08   06 05 04 03 02 01 00 99

One morning, Minerva Louise woke up
before everyone else.

It was a beautiful morning, so she decided
to go for a walk through the tall grass.

She walked on and on.

Oh, look! A big, fancy barn,
thought Minerva Louise.

She watched the farmer hang
his laundry out to dry . . .

. . . and she noticed that he had
left the door open.

So many stalls! There must be
all kinds of animals here.

Here are milking stools for the cows

and a pen for the pigs.

Oh, a bucket, too. It must be
for feeding the chickens.

Nesting boxes! How wonderful!

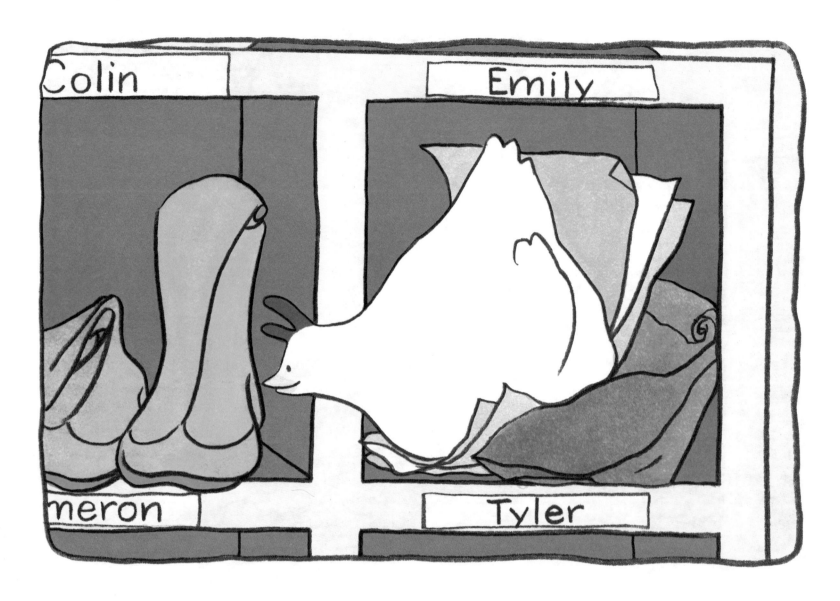

Look at them all. And each one
is decorated differently.

14

This one is all done up with ribbons.

And this one is lined with fur.

Oh my goodness, there's an EGG in this one!

But where is his mother? He'll get cold.

Well, this hay will keep you warm.

I'm sure the animals are around here somewhere. But I have to go home now.

Minerva Louise hurried home
through the tall grass.

She had some work to do.

But she knew she'd go back to the
fancy barn some day . . .

because it was such a wonderful
place to get new ideas.